Y0-BVQ-804

Winifred

Winifred

Written by
Anita Abramovitz

Illustrated by
Carroll Dolezal

STECK-VAUGHN COMPANY • AUSTIN, TEXAS
An Intext Publisher

ISBN 0-8114-7723-1
Library of Congress Catalog Card Number 78-141574

Copyright © 1971 by Steck-Vaughn Company, Austin, Texas
All Rights Reserved
Printed and Bound in the United States of America

Winifred made things,
    all kinds of things,
    anything at all,
    old things, new things,
    big things, and small things.

Winifred made so many things,
she made them all so fast,
they turned out, every one of them,
lopsided, wobbly, squiggly,
rumpled, runny, streaky,
upside down, or inside out.

6

Winifred gave all the things away as presents to everyone who lived on her street.

But no one knew what to do with them. Everyone said, "Thank you," but Winifred was unhappy because no one really meant it.

7

One day the lady next door said,
"Winifred, dear, I know you are clever,
and I know you want to make things
people can use. Why not make signs?"

"Signs," said Winifred,
"what a good idea!"

8

Winifred never wasted time.
The next trip the family took
to the country, Winifred looked
and looked to see what there was
to see in the way of signs.

When she got home, Winifred sat
right down and went to work.

GO SLOW

DAVE'S
HAMBURGER STAND

FRESH
EGGS

HOUSE
for
rent

NO
U
TURN

DOVER-20 MILES

STOP

DETOUR

Dangerous
CURVE

ROAD
CLOSED

But nobody could use the signs.
In fact, nobody wanted them at all,
so Winifred put up the signs around
her house.

12

Soon, strangers stopped in for eggs
or hamburgers. They asked about buying
the house.

They stopped at all hours.

Can you imagine what it was like?
Everyone got cross and shouted at
Winifred—so she took down all the
signs and put them into the garbage can.

But that was not the end of it. Once Winifred got started on anything, she couldn't stop. Every time she saw a sign, she had to make one like it.

STORAGE CO.

1451

ROOM for RENT

SHIRTS 35¢

LEE'S LAUNDRY

OPEN MON. thru SAT.

DRY CLEAN

NO PARK-ING

WALK ONLY IN CROSSWALK

15

Winifred took a trip to the zoo.
When she got back, she sat right down
to make signs.

16

Nobody wanted these signs, either,
so Winifred put the signs here and there,
up and down the street.

What a sight!
There were red and purple, gold and
orange signs everywhere.

19

The next morning,
   what an uproar!
   What a rumpus!
   What a racket!
Winifred looked out her window.

There was the fire engine.
There was the ambulance.

There was the police chief.
He looked angry.
    Policemen were pulling down
and tearing up all of Winifred's signs.

And there was Miss Jessica Jones,
the lady next door, lying flat on
the ground.

Winifred wanted to run.
Winifred wanted to hide.
Winifred wanted to fly away.
But she did none of these things.

24

She called from her window,
"Wait! Wait! Wait!"
Quickly and bravely Winifred went down
the stairs, out the door, and said,
"I'm sorry! I'm so sorry, everybody!
I didn't mean to frighten anyone."

25

Then the lady next door sat up
from her faint and told Winifred
that everything was all right.

After that, Winifred helped Miss Jones into her house.

The police left. They took the signs with them, of course.

The fire engine and the ambulance drove away.

Winifred never wasted time.
She got out cardboard, pen, and ink.
She made the biggest sign she had
ever made.

A friend helped Winifred tack her
new sign onto the front porch.

Soon, Winifred was busier than ever.
You never saw such wonderful signs
as Winifred made.
Her first was an order for
Bill Fillman's tree house.

1425

Sleeping
Do Not
DISTURB

BELL
OUT OF
ORDER

Then, a sign in a big hurry for the house
down the street.

Next, a pretty pink sign for her best friend.

And, just last week, Winifred made the
smallest sign she had ever made—a sign for
Miss Jones to put on the collar of her cat.
It had his name on it.

Now everyone says, "Thank you, thank you."
And Winifred is happy because they really
mean it!